This book belongs to

_____

The Adventures of
Bella & Harry
Let's Visit Barcelona!

Written By
Lisa Manzione

Illustrated By
Kristine Lucco

Bella & Harry, LLC

www.BellaAndHarry.com
email: BellaAndHarryGo@aol.com

"Vámonos!"

"What are you saying Bella?"

"Harry, 'vámonos' means 'let's go' in the Spanish language, so... let's go!"

5

Today we are in Barcelona, Spain wandering through Las Ramblas with our family. Las Ramblas is an area in Barcelona lined with cafés, street performers, and all sorts of sights and sounds of this city.

6

WELCOME TO BARCELONA

"**Bella,** look at me! I am running around in a circle!"

"Harry, don't be silly! Do you know who painted this circle?"

"Nope, but running in a circle is a lot of fun!"

"Harry, this is the 'Miró'. It was created by Joan Miró. He was a famous sculptor and painter from Spain."

10

"**Like** many other cities in Europe, Barcelona has many famous artists and famous places to visit. Next stop... Park Guell. We are off to see the 'Gaudi Dragon'!"

"**Bella,** I am afraid of dragons!"

"Harry, it is not a real dragon. The dragon is made of beautiful mosaic tile. The dragon is at the entrance of the famous park created by Antoni Gaudi."

12

"**Gaudi** was a famous architect. An architect is someone who builds and designs things."

"I am going to grow up and be an architect one day, Bella! I want to design things!"

"Okay, Harry! When you grow up you can be anything you want to be, but right now we are off to see another Gaudi building! Next stop... Sagrada Familia!"

"**Harry!** Sagrada Familia is one of the most visited sights in Barcelona. Sagrada Familia is a religious site. It is a church."

14

"**The** church is very interesting, Harry. The church was not started by Antoni Gaudi, but Gaudi had great ideas about what it should look like when finished, so he started working on the project too."

"**Come** on Harry! We can climb to the top of one of the towers. We will have a great view of the city. Be careful while climbing the stairs... and don't run, Harry!!!"

16

"Harry, look! We have a perfect view of the spires (or tower tops) of Sagrada Familia."

17

"**It** was Gaudi's idea that the church have 18 towers. The towers are different in both size and shape. The tallest tower is approximately 558 feet high... or 558 cats...tail to tail!"

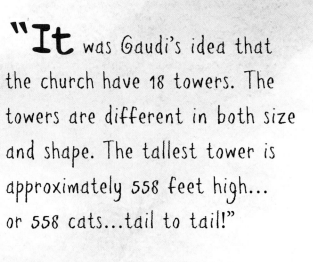

18

Suddenly, Bella saw a butterfly and did not remember what she told Harry. Bella started to run!

"Harry, look! A butterfly!"

"**Bella,** look out! There is a paint can on the step!"

Bump... Bump!!! Bump... Bump!!!

"Bella! Are you okay?"

"**Yes** Harry, I am okay! I forgot this was a construction site. I should have been more careful."

"Ha! Ha! Bella, you look funny with blue paint on your paws!"

21

"Vamos a almorzar!"

"Bella, what are you saying? You know I don't speak Spanish!"

"Vamos a almorzar means let's go to lunch! I need to rest my paws after tumbling down the stairs."

22

Restaurante

MENÚ ESPECIAL

Gazpacho
(Cold tomato soup)

Tortilla Española
(Spanish omelet)

Chorizo
(Spanish pork sausage)

Flan
(Vanilla custard with
caramel sauce)

"**Harry,** look! The children are having 'tapas'."

"Bella, what does 'tapas' mean?"

"**Well** Harry, tapas is a wide variety of snacks or little meals."

"I love snacks, Bella!"

"I think the meal today consists of cheese, meat, peppers and tortillas."

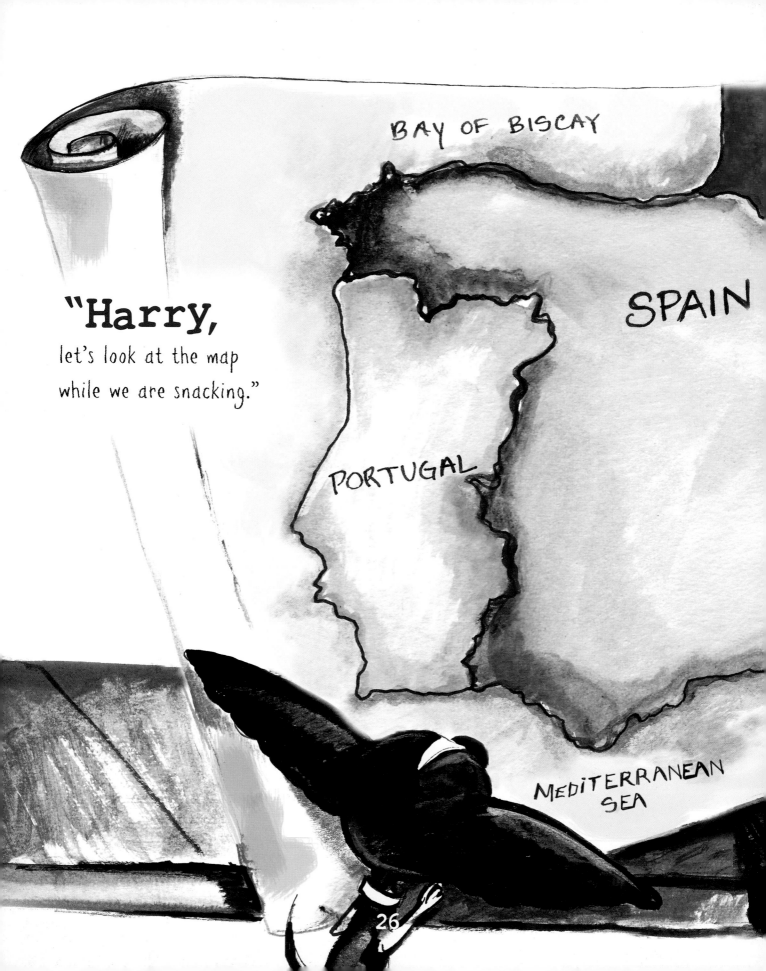

FRANCE

BARCELONA

"**See,** Harry? We are right here. Barcelona is the capital of Catalonia, a region within the country of Spain. There are seventeen regions within the country of Spain."

"Time to go. Snack time is over."

"Casa Batlló is our next stop on our tour. Isn't this cool, Harry? The outside of the building is made of tiny bits of glass and mosaic tile. The stone columns look like bones and the balconies look like masks! The top of the house looks like scales or the back of a dragon!"

28

"**Harry,** Casa Batlló was also built by Antoni Gaudi. The house is now a museum. I love museums. I know you do too Harry!"

29

"**Bella,** I know where we are going next."

"Where are we going, Harry?"

"Montserrat! We are going to take a funicular,
or cable car ride, to the tippy top of the mountain."

"**You** are correct, Harry! Next stop... the top of a very high mountain! Once we arrive at the top of the mountain, we will have great views of Barcelona."

"Wow! What a beautiful view! We can see all of the Catalonian countryside. Shh... do you hear the music, Harry? The music is being sung by the choir boys in the Monastery. The choir sings almost every day at 1:00 pm."

"What beautiful music! Spain is a very interesting place to visit, Bella!"

Well, as you can see, we had a great time in Spain but it is time to return home. Who knows where we are off to next! As long as you join us, we know it will be fun! For now it is... Hasta luego, mi amigo... or Good-bye, my friend... from Bella Boo and Harry too!

Our Adventure to Barcelona

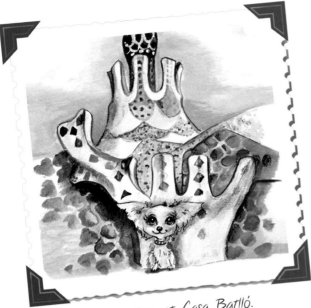

Bella posing at Casa Batlló.

Harry enjoying paella. A traditional Spanish dish made with rice and seafood.

Playing chase in Park Guell.

Playing soccer.

Beautiful art in Barcelona!

Bella & Harry visiting a flower shop.

Common Spanish Words and Phrases

Cat – Gato

Dog – Perro

Boy – Niño

Girl – Niña

What time is it? – Que hora es?

What is your name? – Cuál es tu nombre?

Do you speak Spanish? – Hablas español?

No, I do not speak Spanish. – No, yo no hablo español.

Good morning – Buenos dias

Good afternoon – Buenas tardes

Good evening – Buenas noches

Requests for permission to make copies of any part of the work should be directed to BellaAndHarryGo@aol.com or 855-235-5211.

Library of Congress Cataloging-in-Publications Data is available

Manzione, Lisa

The Adventures of Bella & Harry: Let's Visit Barcelona!

ISBN: 978-1-937616-06-9

First Edition

Book Six of Bella & Harry Series

For further information please visit:

www.BellaAndHarry.com

or

Email: BellaAndHarryGo@aol.com

CPSIA Section 103 (a) Compliant

www.beaconstar.com/consumer

ID: L0118329. Tracking No.: L1412424-8244

Printed in China